RITA AND THE RANGE

To Ahan for being so patient, sticking around, and encouraging me.

"Real or Unreal?"
"Fact or Dream?"

CONTENTS

PREFACE

Adventure and Fantasy make a great combination. A middle schooler has so many things on her mind. The world from her eyes is an exciting piece of a big puzzle. Seeking challenge and fighting emotions in a weird world makes an interesting story.

RITA AND THE RANGE

Ashmi Sengupta

THE REBEL

Once upon a time, in Spring Valley, Arizona, lived an adventurous and fierce girl named Marita Joanne Lopez. Marita, also known as Rita, was twelve, just into middle school, and had dreams, brave and adventurous. She lived in a world of her own making, a world of fantasy, unbelievable characters where she was a lone fighter against all else. So naturally, the natural world seemed alien to her. Rita didn't like her parents, or even the cute 6-year-old pet cat, Teriyaki, although she was kind of her only little friend. As usual, Rita was always bored at home, so she spent most of her time in her room, petting Teriyaki, reading, and finishing her homework.

It was a small place, and people practically knew each other. Strangers were rare. Fall was here, and the weather was significantly cooler. The northern part of the town had a beautiful township called Ellie's Green. The word green was because the entire gated community was nice and green overlooking the valley which lay ahead.

Ellie's Green Apartments was a small withdrawn community where all kids knew each other, and Rita was no one's favorite. Every day after school, the bus dropped her off at her building number Seven. Rita would bang her feet up the steel stairs, knock on the door, and when her mother opened the door, she stomped in with her muddy shoes. Then, straight, she would go to her room. Washing her hands was a reasonable daily regimen. After that, reading was next. After that, homework and Papa's math were just "optional."

At times from her room, not even thinking about what she was saying, she shouted, "I JUST HATE THE WORLD!!!!"

One afternoon Rita was usually stomping into the house with her muddy sneakers on, ignoring Mama's worries about, especially, dirty shoes in the house, ignoring Papa's comments on getting 35% on her Tagalog test, went straight to her pale blue room. Rita took off her white sneakers and socks, then took off the hot pink jacket, curled up in her bed, observing her creative writing. Then she sulked sadly.

She had some homework from Ms. Minny, her ELA teacher. She had asked her to interview an older person. Rita was just not in the mood. She had thought of visiting Mrs. Clayton in her community or maybe even one of her parents. But No! She kind of hated them all. Why? She couldn't find any reason. Is a reason necessary? Huh! Forget about it.

Days turned routine, and evenings were super dull. She didn't like to talk to anyone. Everyone ignored her. Until one day, Rita had enough. She grabbed two backpacks and shoved in a water bottle, her phone, a charger, a book, and some other things.

Papa was at work, busy with his never-ending meetings. Mama was in the kitchen balancing a lasagna tray in one hand and a phone in another. She was dialing a number. Rita got a chance. She stormed out of the little room, grabbed inquisitive Teriyaki, shoved her backpacks on her back, abandoned her school, and seized her teal bicycle. She headed off to the desert road, ashamed and angry. While she was getting on the bike, she whispered to herself, "Mama and Papa, what else could I do?"

Willa Manchester lived on the opposite side of Rita's apartment. Whenever Rita walked out of the door or walked inside her room, the bossy neighbor, Willa Manchester, stuck her neck out and watched her.

She shrugged and closed her door—no big deal.

THE DESERT

Ashmi Sengupta

The cold afternoon wind swooshed against her hair. Rita was pedaling as hard as she could. She was! Her feet were tired, but she didn't stop. Phew! The little bike basket was bothering Teriyaki. It was uncomfortable and a bumpy ride. Teriyaki scratched and growled and hissed and scratched and howled and purred inquisitively, but Rita paid no attention to him. Tears came into her eyes. The streets became emptier, and she reached a barren land. Dusk was approaching. "What else could I do, Teriyaki?" she exclaimed. "STOP IT, TERI~."

Suddenly, something bothered her. Was that a tickle? It could be. Or maybe it was just her imagination. No. Rita skidded to a stop. She pulled herself off the bike and looked around everywhere. She could hear a faint stirring under her, but she ignored that. She was concentrating on the tickle.

"What's happening, Teriyaki?" she asked to no one in particular. She didn't know Teriyaki had escaped. He probably wondered if the Mad Hatter or something would attack him. Enough of that. Now Rita felt a bit scared. A bit more skittish than usual. Now Rita understood what was happening.

There was a slight rumbling sound originating from the barrens. Rita parked her bike with the kickstand and slowly walked to investigate. "C'mon Teriyaki," she said. She saw a rocky mound, and the vibrations were coming from there. She walked carefully one step at a time, Teriyaki in her arms. The vibrations continued....

A little scared, she stretched her finger and poked a rock. Suddenly there was an explosion of stones; Rita was covered in dirt. The ground shook like crazy. Rita was struggling to see what was going on. She heard a roar and a shriek; it sounded like a killer whale she heard on National Geographic. Slowly she wiped her eyes, and she looked around and shrieked in horror. "A GARGANTUAN LAND-LIVING OCTOPUS!!!"

This was the shock of her life. Octopuses are supposed to live in the oceans, right? But that one was in a desert, thousands and thousands of miles away from an ocean.

Eyes angry and evil, saliva dripping from its mouth, the thing looked at Rita as if it had been disturbed from its sleep. Rita was terrified. She pinched herself. "Wake up! Wake up! This is a bad dream!" But it was not. Slowly the octopus slithered towards Rita, one of its tentacles drawing closer. This SUBSTANTIAL, slimy, lewd, azure-blue tentacle poked Rita in the spines. Then about three more appeared and grabbed Rita. They weaved themselves up and jammed Rita. Rita thought she was going to end up like an orange.

She managed to take out her hand from the grip of the octopus.

Rita tackled the octopus for some hours (or it seemed like many hours) with just a broken branch which she managed to pull out of a dead tree, and then Rita suddenly had the instinct to reach behind her back. She then pulled out a bunch of arrows and a bow. But how could she pull out a bow and arrow? After that, she had an idea. She would attack the octopus with her bows and arrows. She was ready! Rita was anxious, but she was determined to complete the task. The massive, creepy, and hideous octopus scraped its tentacles on Rita. She was terrified, and she felt she had found 80 of those arrows. She bought them at the weapon store (or did she? She was just 12. How could Rita? God! Rita couldn't remember where she got them from).

She looked at her feet, and she had combat boots on. She bought them from a thrift store a year back and stuffed them in her closet. Huh! This seemed somewhat enchanted. "Enough! Focus on the colossal octopus". She somehow grabbed her Bow with one hand, and with another, she grabbed a handful of Arrows. Some hideous tentacles tightly clasped her feet. With great effort, Rita shot 8 of her arrows one by one into each tail-ish hand and one indicator straight into the pupil of its eyes. How did she learn archery? She felt confused, but more on that later. The octopus gradually released the tight clasp and fell limp. Finally, after dealing with the colossal octopus, which now lay defeated in the barren land, Rita was in the desert with Teriyaki.

The night was dark, and it was getting colder. Rita was tired and hungry. She drew out cactus water with her little knife from her emergency kit in her bag and plucked out many berries. Finally, the night was gone, and a day passed. The days seemed boring. Rita was all alone. She felt like on a deserted island. Well, she *did* have her dad's credit card. But no place to use it. And ever since then, Rita realized that life was   full   of   impossibilities. Rita didn't like the desert. She wanted her family back. She wanted her house back—even bossy Willa. Teriyaki was surprisingly dull. What else could I do? were the only words hovering over her head. What else could I do? What else could I do? Rita knew there were desert dangers here. Days were spent in extreme heat, meows, and prickly cactuses.

Nights were frigid and scary. She took off her sneakers and sighed. Then she grabbed her phone. She tried to contact Mama, but there was no signal. It was late afternoon, and her hands were as cold as ice. It was mid-October, and temperatures were dropping. Teriyaki was fast asleep. Rita fished in her backpack and found extra clothing. She felt something hard in it. Her mind felt curious. She took out a small dime and a photo of Mama and Papa. She wanted to sob, but she didn't. There was noise. Yes, she heard something. It could be someone. But, the thing was, who was it? Rita felt a shiver down her spine. Hmmm, maybe it just was her imagination. But no. Not the concept of the colossal octopus. No. No. NO!

THE NEW GIRL

Rita turned around, made a slight noise on the slippery dirt, and saw another girl. The girl was about 11, standing about six feet away with a curious look. She smiled but nervously. Rita smiled back like a fool. The smiling seemed to go on forever. But who was she, a kind of ghost? Well, she *could* be.

The girl wore khaki pants, a floral top, and long and beautiful hair. She was tall and steady. She also had gleaming and curious eyes. She was beautiful. Suddenly, behind her came a terrified face. The face belonged to a very young boy. He looked like 6 or 7, not much older than that. The girl finally broke the silence by saying, "Hi! My name is Flora. What is your name?" All Rita could manage was, "M-m-my name is R-Rita." Flora asked, "Do you have any siblings? This is Nathaniel, or Ned for short. He doesn't bug me, though. So who is your sibling again?"

"I-I don't have siblings." Rita's voice trembled. She then blurted out, "Are *you* a ghost?" Rita wished that those words didn't float out of her mouth. "I'm sorry and, er-" Rita's voice trailed off. What was she saying? Flora said, "That's okay. Come on, let's visit my house," Rita said, "Your house? We're in the middle of nowhere! " Flora smiled and replied, " Trust me," Rita followed the siblings. She hadn't walked more than ten paces when Ned squealed, "I don't think I trust her, Flora." Rita looked at Flora desperately, and Flora looked at her with steady caramel eyes and *finally* spoke, "I trust her." Rita followed Flora. After a couple of hundred yards, lights came out of nowhere, and she saw a beautiful oasis and a cozy little cottage by it. Flora smiled and said, " C'mon in," Rita followed her and entered the warmth of the neat little cottage. Flora grabbed her arm and took her to the kitchen. "I'm hungry," said Flora, "let's smash and crush some potatoes and dump them in the heating bowl. Let's surprise our parents. Oh well, look behind, here are my parents!" she cheerfully declared. Behind Flora, two happy-looking people arrived with smiles and joy on their faces. Ned, in the meantime, ran out in a hurry.

Ashmi Sengupta

FLAWLESS
PARENTS

The parents were very cheerful. Flora introduced them by saying, "This is my father Bob Hawkings, and I call him Pa." "This is Esther Hawkings," she explained again, pointing to her mother. "I call her Mãma." Her Pa looked tall and sturdy, just like his daughter. He wore navy blue glasses, a vintage green shirt, and a smile. His shoes were smudged with mud and dirt, just like Rita's. His pants, though, were shiny and were creased with every lining. Her Mãma was a little stubby, wearing a knee-high flowered skirt showing her tan, thick legs. However, she also wore a smile like Flora's Pa. Her shirt was a bit dirty. It was actually like a tee, with shoulder-length sleeves. Her shirt was scarlet.

Flora's Pa, or for now called Mr. Hawkings, asked, "Hi! What's your name?" Rita started to say her name when a screaming Ned interrupted, "WAAH! Woah!" Flora almost tripped by running out of the cottage, but Mr. and Mrs. Hawkings didn't run. They didn't even move. Mr. and Mrs. Hawkings were perfectly flawless. Somehow, they managed to not care about their screaming child, Nathaniel, or called Ned. Mrs. Hawking announced, "Nothing is going to happen. Relax." Just then, Ned ran in, screaming," Mãma! Pa! There is a most enormous rainbow I've ever seen!" Flora then suggested, "Let's go outside and see the rainbow," Everyone agreed and headed outside. The Flawless Parents echoed: "Don't say that I didn't tell you to relax,"

TERIYAKI'S ANTICS

Ashmi Sengupta

Teriyaki was on the ground, and he growled at Mrs. Hawkings. Mr. Hawkings coughed and then crooned, " I see you have a cat with you". Meanwhile, Mrs. Hawkings was creeping backward, her flowery blue skirt flowing behind her. Rain was rare in the area, but it had rained last night, and the soil was wet. Her shoes were getting muddy by the minute, and she almost tripped over a brown rock.

"Mãma! Where are you going? Mãma! Mãma! Mãma! Stop! Remember your doctor said to-" Flora's voice trailed off into the cliffs. Rita asked, "What did you say, Flora?" Flora or Ned didn't talk. Teriyaki was attacking their parents. "Teriyaki! Teriyaki! Stop it, now! Teriyaki! Bad cat! Bad cat! Stop it Teriyaki!" Rita's hollers were no use. The growling cat still hypnotized Mr. and Mrs. Hawkings. Rita was desperate to save them.

Teriyaki was chasing them. Something was happening to him! Each of his pounces was a yard long. Mr. and Mrs. Hawkings were rushing like crazy!! Flora sprinted behind them. Rita skidded around Teriyaki, hoping to catch them. "God, save us, please!" shouted Flora. Teriyaki suddenly stopped. He didn't seem to move. Rita grabbed him by the tail. "If you come, dear inquisitive Teriyaki, I'll give you a fish, and a jolly good one!" With the word "fish", Teriyaki started to drool. He was SO engaged with the fish he began to walk toward Rita.

Ashmi Sengupta

THE PLAN

Rita apologized to the Hawkings' family after the Teriyaki incident. They slowly walked back to their home. The five of them sat on couches in the living room. The heat from the old radiator was comforting. Teriyaki was lapping milk from a bowl, much more in control. Mrs. Hawkings made hot chocolate for the kids. Rita was sipping on the drink, and tears came to her eyes. "What's wrong, Rita?" asked Mrs. Hawkings. "I left my home," sobbed Rita, "I was angry at my parents and just left on my bike. I don't know where I am. I miss my parents," added Rita.

"We can help you, dear, where d'you live?" asked Mr. Hawkings.

Rita had no idea what to say. All she remembered was her town name and some landmark. "Spring Valley," she answered. "My home is a white and teal building, five blocks from my school"

"What's your school name?" asked Mr. Hawkings. "Desert Ridge Academy," said Rita.

"Mmmm..."

Mr. Hawkings pulled out his map book and started looking. "I have a plan. You have come very far off, Rita,"

Rita wasn't listening. She had an idea. She could *find* her way back! *But that would be too hard,* thought Rita. *I might just have to ask for help,* thought Rita again. Rita walked over to Flora and Ned. "I might just need some extra help from you guys." Flora answered, "Of course!" Ned, though, didn't want to help Rita with whatever she was going to do, but eventually, he agreed. The Hawkings was eager to help. Teriyaki bounced up and down. "It's a long trip. We are all coming with you. Spring Valley would be nice at this time of the year," Said Mrs. Hawkings. Finally, they all were ready to go.

Mrs. Hawkings screamed, "Pack up, everybody!" So Mr. Hawkings packed a change of clothes, toothbrush and toothpaste, new shoes, his Kindle, and a lunchbox of bread and butter.

Mrs. Hawkings packed a couple of flowery skirts, a toothbrush, her change of dresses, new shoes, a lunchbox of bread and jam, her paints, paper, and her ever-ready medical supply box (yes, they had medicines). Flora packed a change of clothes, her diary and pencil, toothbrush (of course), her crayons and notebook, three books, and her lunchbox of bread, mashed potatoes, and cheddar cheese. *Rita hated cheddar cheese.* Ned packed his teddy bear, his change of clothes, a lunchbox full of animal crackers, a water bottle, his toothbrush, his favorite books, a stinky tuna sandwich, his toys, and his extra reading glasses.

At last, Rita just grabbed her backpack. She peeked in her backpack: A toothbrush and her toothpaste, new shoes, her fluffy hot pink jacket, her homework, and last, a picture of Mama and Papa and she, standing in front of her birthday present on her third birthday, a cute light-blue teddy. She thought all of these would help her set up a new life, but here we go. She put the backpack on top of her bike seat.

THE SURPRISE

Rita and her friends started on their adventure back home. But not quite. They did have a map, yes, but the map went blank. They didn't know, after all, that the map was a *moving map*. A moving map is something that moves with every single location it goes. So, for example, if you're in Las Vegas, NV, right now, then the map will show Las Vegas, NV. Now, if you want to go from Las Vegas, NV, to Henderson, NV, then the map will show the directions to Henderson, NV.

At last, it was time to investigate their moving map. Everyone was ready to be investigating. After all, they were all, for now, *temporary detectives.* But not seriously, of course. Ned was the first to holler out, "I got clues, everyone!" Everyone turned to Ned, who was turning a slimy green. "Er, uh - " Ned pointed behind Rita. Two yellow lights came from a distance, and a soft roar got louder. From the dirt road, a yellow Chevrolet Silverado approached. Mr. Hawkings held out his hand and stuck out his thumb. The truck screeched to a stop. A gentle white-haired lady with glass spectacles peeked out from the driver's seat.

Rita was shocked! It was the face of Denise Clayton! Denise Grace Clayton was the old lady next door to Lopez's back home. "Mrs. Clayton !!!" exclaimed Rita.

"Rita! What in the world are you doing here? Your parents are worried sick back home," squealed Mrs. Clayton.

"How did you get here?" asked Rita sharply.

"Well, I just thought I would follow your bike tread marks when your parents told me about your escape. I have headed over to Black Canyon City anyways, and look! I found you," said Mrs. Clayton, rather skittishly.

The Hawkings looked relieved, but Flora looked sad, and Ned smiled.

"Hop in," said Mrs. Clayton.

The Hawkings had a blank expression on their faces. "It's alright, Sir, Madame," said Mrs. Clayton. "I'll take care of Rita. I'll take her back home to her parents. Thanks so much for all you've done, folks."

THE LETTER

Rita opened the front door, but Mrs. Clayton said, "Dear, sit in the back seat, sorry for any inconvenience, sorry, never mind, please," Rita simply closed the door and said, "Yeah, yeah, that's okay," The bike went on the back.

Rita waved bye to her new friends, so did Flora. However, Flora felt a little sad to see her friend go and miss all the adventure.

The truck started on its way on the dirt road. "Here you go, dear, this is for you,"

Mrs. Clayton handed a piece of scrunchy paper to Rita.

Rita took the paper with trembling hands. What was written here?

" *'Dear daughter,*

I know that you left the house in a storm of anger. I apologize deeply for any inconvenience. I am just very depressed that my actual part of life has left my life. I am sorry, as I am saying again.' I don't think you mean that word, mother.

Stay safe, my precious, signed by your dear mother, Kiya.' ''

Rita felt a little sad and started crying, she was really missing her parents now, and she was glad to return home. She didn't realize that the truck had stopped.

Ashmi Sengupta

THE PACKAGES

Rita raised her head and asked, "Mrs. Clayton, why did we stop?" Then she got the shock of her life. There was no one in the driver's seat.

Rita shouted, "Mrs. Clayton, Mrs. Clayton!!" She looked out the window, and there was no one. Now, what is happening? The road was deserted. Rita was scared. She said a prayer, got down, and went to the back of the truck. No one here too.

She waited for about an hour, but there was no one, and there was no signal on her phone yet. So she took down her bike from the truck and her backpack too. The backpack, too, was heavier than usual, but *how* could that be?

Rita was feeling very confused. Was Mrs. Clayton real, or did she see a ghost? But her friends also saw her, right? Rita looked back and got another shock. The truck had disappeared.

Rita started crying and felt afraid now. "Mom!" she called. "Where are you?" Then, finally, she heard a sound from her backpack, and she stopped crying.

She opened her bag and found two mysterious packages in it.

"Now, what's in these packages?"

The first package contained a... before Rita could think, the package *opened by **itself***. It was one of those talking parakeets. The parakeet wanted a name, so Rita named her Natasha. The parakeet chirped, "She's a girl, she's a girl," The second one contained a small eight by ten sketchbook with a pencil and a pencil sharpener, a lilac-colored eraser, and a note saying: *Have fun with those, dear!*

"Oh, I will," sighed Rita, sighing again and feeling even weirder.

DANEEN.

Rita sat down on the road, not knowing what to do. The parakeet kept on chirping, "She's a girl, she's a girl,"

"I know I'm a girl," argued Rita annoyingly, swinging the cage so the parakeet would stop chirping. Then, Rita realized that the parakeet wasn't looking at her. Instead, it was looking behind her.

Rita turned to see a younger girl than herself. She was just like looking into a mirror, a younger Rita!

Rita looked at the dreamy eyes of the girl who was in front of her. She looked faded, like she had been covered in cream-colored dust, only she wasn't.

"Hi," said Rita, gazing into the girl's beauty.

"Hello, Rita," said the girl dreamily. She was wearing a dirty soccer jersey with the number 8 peeling onto it. Her shorts were yellow & orange. She had a scrummy Band-Aid on her knees.

"Why are you looking at me like that?" asked Rita, trembling a bit. Those dreamy eyes were drilling into

Rita's eyes.

"Stop it!" repeated Rita, now trembling even more.

"She's weird," muttered Rita, turning away.

"Excuse me," said the girl. Her voice was not dreamy right now, and so were her eyes. "I think I heard you say 'weird.'"

"Okay," said Rita slowly, turning around to face the mysterious girl. "You have a great ear, I guess. I mean, who'd-"

"Excuse me," repeated the girl. Her voice wasn't dreamy now. "Who were you saying weird to?"

"You," Rita blurted out. She turned a bit pink.

"Okay," said the girl slowly. "You have a great voice, I guess. I mean, who would-"

"Woah, woah, woah, stop right there," interrupted Rita, smirking. "You just said the same thing I did,"

"No, I did not," said the girl, grinning, losing even more of her dreaminess. "I said that you have a great voice,"

"Oh, thanks," said Rita, not believing that a girl younger than her could be so bright. "Who are you, anyway?" added Rita.

"*Maybe you have a secret,*" said the girl silently.

"Who are you, what kind of secret are you talking about, what're you doing here?" asked Rita, getting more surprised at how this girl appeared from no-where.

"I'm Belladonna," the girl whispered, smiling slightly.

"Er- hi, Belladonna," said Rita. "What are you doing here?" she added.

"Don't you know, Rita? I'm your destiny and your future," said Belladonna, "Come to Daneen if you don't believe me,"

"Wait-wait-wait. I have some questions. How'd you know my name? And are you sure that you're my destiny and future?" asked Rita suspiciously.

"Come to Daneen with me," whispered the girl again mysteriously.

"Daneen *what*? Can you go away for a moment? I need to get things straight," mumbled Rita.

Belladonna stopped talking. Rita thought about her memories. Her mother would feed her fresh goats' milk. At the age of 1-3, she was fed a nutritious paste that tasted like chocolate. At the age of 4-7, she ate wheat & honey bread with pure butter. She bathed in rose water and washed with lilac-scented soap. *Aaah*, she imagined. But Belladonna's sentence kept on ringing inside her head. *Come to Daneen with me. Come to Daneen with me.*

Somehow she remembered Daneen. It was a vague memory from her childhood, a magical place, which she couldn't remember what that place meant. "I shall go to Daneen," she said firmly to herself, absent-mindedly. She called, "BELLADONNA!"

"Why'd you call me?" asked a voice.

Rita suddenly realized that Belladonna was talking. Then something snapped through her mind. She answered, "I called you so I'd tell you that I'm going to Daneen and also-"

"Rita! Are you *serious*?" exclaimed Belladonna. She started with a chuckle. Then she giggled. Then she squealed. Then she chortled. "Could you stop laughing? I have to hurry. I don't have much time..." muttered Rita annoyingly and hurriedly. But Belladonna didn't listen. She kept on laughing. Ha, ha, ha. Someone's going to some kind of Daneen place, and her companion is laughing her head out? Not. Funny.

"BELLADONNA! ARE YOU LISTENING TO ME! BELLA! ARE YOU LISTE-"

Belladonna stopped laughing. She froze. She wasn't even blinking. "Did you call me *Bella*?" she asked after what seemed like a million centuries later. "Yes," snapped Rita. "Any problem with that?"

At first, Belladonna didn't believe that Rita was *so* rigid and strict.

Then she whispered, "No," But then she said rather rudely, "You know what? A *coward* like *you* would never *deserve* to go to a place as *posh* as my homeland, *Daneen*. Hmph!"

Rita looked awestruck. Then she slowly said, "Okay. At first, I didn't even *want* to go. But you? You are forcing me to go there!"

But Belladonna didn't stop her eagerness. She quietly said, "Come to Daneen with me,"

THE PASS

.

Ashmi Sengupta

Dear Marita Joanne Lopez, Greetings from Daneen! I welcome you warmly to our homeland. Here, there are buffets for only 5 cents, a pretty landscape called The Jufiyer Demesne, *where you can bathe in its turquoise waters, and drink refreshing lemonade while sunbathing, licking on a cone of exquisite specialty* Jufiyer Demesne *raspberry and chocolate chip ice-cream; go to the* Jufiyer Demesne Spa and Salon *to get your nails done and your hair made into the traditional Daneen style; you can buy rainbow-colored woolen scarves, jackets, pants and shirts, all Daneen special. There are also lots and lots of hotels, especially the most famous one,* The Golden Beach; Hotel and Motel. *Please visit anytime you desire.*

Thanks and Regards,

Nicholas Timothy Poloman

YOU MAY ENTER DANEEN

UT INTRARET DANEEN

WHERE DID
SHE GO?

"So, er- is this my pass to enter Daneen?" asked Rita curiously. "Yes," answered Belladonna, grinning.

"Welcome to Daneen. We speak Latin, usually," she added. Rita pushed her bike along with Teriyaki on the bike seat while Belladonna started walking. "How far is Daneen?" asked Rita. "In a bit, you just need to be patient," replied Belladonna. They approached a dense cactus plantation almost 10 feet high. Rita had never seen cacti so tall. Belladonna was smiling. Rita was cautious. They entered the little cactus forest, and it was a dark walk inside.

After about ten minutes, they exited the bushes and what she saw was amazing.

Daneen!! It *was* pretty beautiful. Rita did have some money, but it wasn't more than 125 bucks. Rita was very hungry, and Belladonna took her to *Kipler Boots: Buffet & Grill*.

"So, Daneen isn't *as* bad as you thought, is it?" asked Belladonna as Rita scooped up boiled peas and hot potato on her tray. Rita grabbed another tray and shoved some fresh sardines on the tray. She grabbed a hot potato and mashed it with a spoon.

"Maybe not that bad, yeah," admitted Rita, grabbing a piece of fried chicken with her pincers. "Well, well, you did admit it's the best place you've ever gone to," said Belladonna, trying to be reasonable. "I didn't-" started Rita, but she didn't continue to argue. After all, the food was excellent, and she was starving. She now piled up her tray with ketchup and sat down on a stool in front of a tall-ish table for 2.

"So- will you stay with me long enough to-" started Belladonna, sitting on the other stool.

"To do what?" asked Rita, picking up boiled peas with her fork.

Belladonna lowered her voice to a whisper, then said, "To visit my secret hideaway," Rita was confused, and deciding to say nothing, she shoved a lot of potato with her spoon in her mouth and then suddenly choked when Belladonna said, "Right now, you can wander around Daneen. But meet me at 5:15 in the afternoon, in front of this buffet, okay?" Rita shrugged, then nodded. "Okay," she mumbled as she started to rip her piece of fried chicken with her fork. Belladonna had said she wasn't hungry, but she suddenly got up and grabbed a tray from the counter. She returned with her plate full of sliced pineapples, pie, fried fish, sauces, and pizza slices. She now picked up some pieces of pineapples and gobbled them up quickly, then attacked a pizza slice. Rita finished her last peas then went to the cashier to pay 5 cents for her lunch. Rita paid 5 cents for her fried chicken, peas, and potato. Food was cheap. The place was magical indeed!

Rita turned to face Belladonna, but she wasn't there. She'd probably gone away, but there was only one cashier. Wasn't she supposed to be standing behind Rita at the line? She did have to pay, didn't she? Maybe Daneen residents don't have to pay. Possibly Rita could be a Daneen resident, somehow. Rita got confused but then decided to look for her when she was done eating. She decided to grab some dessert before she went away. Rita pulled out a dessert tray and went to the dessert aisle. She took out an orange frosting cupcake with rainbow sprinkles out of a box. Then she took a slice of chocolate cake with turquoise curlicues out of another box. She didn't sit on a stool this time; she stood in a corner and ate it up. She paid another 5 cents to the cashier after she had eaten her dessert.

"Hey, Teriyaki, d'you want to get some sardines? Or a picture of mice?" asked Rita vaguely.

Then Rita got the shock of her life. TERIYAKI WAS GONE.

Rita ran out of the restuarant. She walked through the street ahead and spotted a lady.

"Er ~ Mademoiselle? H-have you've seen an an-an orangish cat with y-yellow stripes?" asked Rita. "Go away, lady!" snapped the woman. "Don't come and ask me! And my name's not 'Mademoiselle,' it's Yvonne! 'And if she had some brain,'" she muttered.

"Okay!" said Rita annoyingly.

"SAM!!!" called out Rita. Maybe there would be some people named Sam. About 5 or 6 people came to her. "Yeah, girl?" said one of the Sams. "We ain't have all day!" Rita was incredulous. She didn't know that people were mean. "Well, have you seen a yellow-and-orange striped cat?" she asked hopefully.

An old Sam came over and said, "Nǐ hǎo, shūnǚ. Wǒ jiào Sam Wú. Wǒ huì bāngzhù nǐ de. Wǒ tīng shuō nàlǐ zhèngzài jǔbàn Jufiyer Demesne zhōngguó xīnnián wǎnhuì. Nǐ kěyǐ qù nàlǐ kàn kàn yǒu méiyǒu qùguò nàlǐ,"

Rita had no idea what Mr. Sam had just said, and she asked the other five Sams, "Er ~ d'you know what Mr. Sam said?" Another very eager Sam said, "Aah, he said that there is a Chinese New Year party going on in the Jufiyer Demesne. Probably your darling cat is there, dear," he added. Rita borrowed a map from Mr. Wú and started. "Okay, so I've got to make a sharp turn to the left and avoid~ WHAT? Shangerdoodles and waglyuts?" Rita was surprised. HUH! "Anyway, avoid those and just go straight until I have reached and that means reached the demesne," Rita started to walk towards the right, and and finally she saw the party. Okay, she could now see the party! She stepped forward to the gang, but then she saw that kitty cats were partying! WOW! This was tremendously cool!! And guess who she saw first? TERIYAKI!! He had put on traditional Chinese wear and had two lai sees (CNY envelopes) with dollars in them. It looked like Teriyaki loved all the fun! Rita said, "Oh, you silly cat! Oh, and if you come with me, then I'll buy you some fresh sardines and a beautiful page of mice. Don't you know that we have a lot of work leftover?"

中国新年快乐!!!

Rita checked her watch. 3:46. There were roughly 2 hours until Belladonna's secret meeting. Rita walked out and started to look for her. But she wasn't anywhere. She first went to check out the spa. She walked all the way there. Then, she went inside to see many people getting their hair and nails done. But no Belladonna. Next, she went to another restaurant named *Misty's*. Many people had a late lunch and a *very* early dinner. But no Belladonna. After that, she went to one of the hotels. She saw some people lounging around and sipping wine. Others were in the swimming pool, talking about stuff. But weirdly, Belladonna *was* with them.

"BELLADONNA!" Rita gasped. "BELLADONNA! I was looking for you practically EVERYWHERE! Why don't you answer me when I ask you a question?" Rita stopped for a second and took a deep breath. "Why'd you escape when I called for you? Why didn't you have to pay at that restaurant? *I* came to Daneen with you! Where are my answers?"

Belladonna didn't show the least sign of importance and continued laughing and gossiping with the others. Some people looked a little bit surprised, but the others didn't pay attention. Now Rita had lost her patience. Anger and fury boiled inside. She grabbed Belladonna by the rim of her top and shrieked, "YOU COME WITH ME!!!" Belladonna now saw Rita and said, "Wait," She climbed out of the swimming pool, soaking wet. But then, she snapped her fingers, and she was dry as ever. Rita blinked twice and pinched herself, but Belladonna? She was perfectly dry. Even Rita was wet from the swimming pool and Belladonna? Dry. *Is she a ghost*? Thought Rita. But something made her go and apologize to Belladonna.

THE
HIDEAWAY

"Er- I-I- I'm sorry, erm- Belladonna," said Rita awkwardly.

"Oh, oh really- and what - and what makes you say so?" asked Belladonna indignantly.

"Erm-, I meant - meant those words, Belladonna. Rotten apples, stinky, and, er - grabbing you by the - erm - collar," said Rita optimistically.

"Well, I, uh, forgive you," said Belladonna. "But still, come visit my hideaway at-"

"At 5:15, I know," countered Rita annoyingly. "You've told me about that a million times, I know." Belladonna nastily grinned at her, then winked. Next, she beckoned Rita to follow her to her hideaway.

Rita felt hot, so she opened up her braids and let the wind whip on her hair and face. Now, she braided a chunk of hair and pinned it together. Now she'd have loose hair and one braid with her as she went. She decided to take a bath, too. She had been wearing the same clothes for about a week or so. She asked

Belladonna, "Where can I take a bath?"

Belladonna replied, "At the *Bathening Parlor*,"

Rita asked Belladonna to take her to the *Bathening Parlor*.

A while later, Rita got out of the door of the *Bathening Parlor*, wearing an embroidered shirt with roses and tunic pants, feeling fresh as ever. She said, "Let's go and visit your hideaway,"

Belladonna smirked. Then she took her through a dark path, on the other side of sunshine. The pebbled path groaned, the wind howled, the clouds cried, and the twigs shivered as the pair made their way through the trail.

Suddenly, lightning struck, and two tall birches fell onto the trail, and a shiny structure appeared in the middle of the trees. It looked like Snow White's stepmother's magic mirror. Like a portal to a mystical land.

Rita approached the thing with caution. Belladonna didn't seem scared. She strolled over to the mirror-like thing. Rita looked at it, and indeed it was her reflection. It only was a bit blurry, and there was some kind of navy-blue background. "Go ahead and touch it," said Belladonna.

"Why?"

"You'll see, it's magical," Belladonna said. Rita lightly touched the center of the mirror. The wind howled like crazy, and Rita's head started spinning in circles. Something was happening. The smiling face of Belladonna was disappearing slowly. She realized that she was getting pulled inside the mirror. "Help!" screamed Rita.

HOME SWEET HOME

Rita felt a hard sting. Her head was spinning. She lifted her head painfully. She was on her apartment stairs. *What happened?* she thought. A hand came to raise her.

"M-Mrs. Clayton!! Are you Denise Clayton? Where am I? Where's B-Belladonna?" exclaimed Rita.

"Who else would it be?" asked Mrs. Clayton happily.

"Why'd you leave me in the desert?" asked Rita. "Where's Teriyaki? W-W-Where's Belladonna? I thought-"

"Teriyaki's okay. But what did you say? Desert? What are you talking about, honey?" Your parents and I were worried sick and looking all over the neighborhood for you! Where were you? It's been 2 hours !!" exclaimed Mrs. Clayton.

"Flora....Daneen...Belladonna" was all Rita could say. She was confused. "But-but how? Only *two* hours? I - I thought I was gone for a week! I - I thought I was still in Daneen!"

Rita realized she was wearing white sneakers, a

lime-green top, a white skirt, and black tights. *But how?* thought Rita. She didn't even have her pair of bow and arrows. Where was her embroidered shirt? Where were her tunic pants?

Mrs. Clayton shook her head delicately and smiled at Rita. Then she said, "I found you sleeping under a tree in Bancroft County Park. Your breathing was very rapid. I saw you, of course, and tried to wake you up. But you didn't wake up, so I decided to take you home. I just carried you and took you back in my truck to your apartment."

Rita turned her head back to see the bike lying on the floor at the bottom of the stairs and Teriyaki running around it like crazy. She knocked at the door, and it opened on the second knock.

One relieved and the other looking squeamish, the parents looked blankly at Rita. Rita looked blankly at them.

THE REUNION

Then Rita did something *unbelievable* and *unimaginable*.

She ran over to her mother and father and embraced them like she'd never met her parents before. Then, she burst into tears and hugged them like anything.

"Oh mom - dad - I'm *so, so, so* sorry, mom. I - I am sorry. I ran away with Teriyaki, and I stormed out of the house. I'm -" Rita started and then couldn't continue. She flooded into sobs and buried her face in her mom's pink shirt. Her mom kissed her, and her father picked her up from Rita's mom and hugged her.

Rita slipped off her shoes and walked onto the soft, squishy doormat her parents had. It felt so relaxing. Rita then walked inside and smelled the beautiful scent of strawberries and cream air freshener. She hugged her mom again and went to her room to take a bath. As the hot water dripped throughout her hair, she thought about how mean she had been. Flora had taught her a lot. She was her only friend besides her parents, and she was so kind. If only she was real, and not a dream...

The shower alarm rang, meaning 10 minutes were down, and Rita tiptoed out of the shower, soaking wet. She dried herself off with a towel and sighed with happiness. She took out fresh pajamas and slipped them on. She loved the soft sensation in herself. She quickly brushed out the tangles in her hair, braided it into two braids, and pinned them with her favorite "R" clips, which her mother had made for her when she was younger. She put on light blue slippers and walked out of her room to the dining room.

Rita sat down, crying. Her mom said softly, "Dear, it is 7:02. You must be starving, dear. Let's get you something warm to eat," She fixed a hot dish of alfredo pasta for her. She also pulled out a slice of cake for her. Rita was famished, and with each soft bite of the delicious pasta and each lick of frosting, she realized how mean and selfish she had been to her parents. *"No more... I'll change for the better. Home is where love and warmth are,"* thought Rita happily.

"Let us go and read a bedtime story together once you are done." said her father kindly.

Rita's mom interrupted her thoughts and said, "Let us go now. You look exhausted." Rita gratefully nodded.

The portable electric fireplace in the bedroom crackled, giving warmth that felt so good. Rita tucked into her blanket and hugged her mom. She felt like she was at just the right place. She now *never* wanted to leave her home. Never. Her dad pulled out a book and started reading softly.

The book started very interestingly:

"Once upon a time, there was a brave and adventurous girl named Ramiya Martinez. Her nickname was Miya. She lived in Summerville, Marizona. She lived over there with her family. She didn't like the world, her parents, or even the cute pet cat, Meriyaki. She lived in a place called Mellie's Green Apartments, a small withdrawn community....."

THE END

ABOUT THE AUTHOR

Ashmi Sengupta

Ashmi is an 11-year-old who has a penchant for adventure and fantasy novels. Along with her school, she is a voracious reader and loves to write in her free time. She also loves to sketch and creates her own illustrations. Since she was around four, reading, writing, and illustrations have been her passion. Finally, her dream of writing a book came true as she touched Eleven. Ashmi lives in Denver, Colorado with her parents and her little brother.

BOOKS BY THIS AUTHOR

Rita And The Range

Made in the USA
Las Vegas, NV
11 November 2022

59180847R00049